THE STORY OF
TONG AND MAI NHIA
A HMONG LEGEND

REWRITTEN BY SHOO CHA

ILLUSTRATED BY JIM MADSEN

Once there were two neighbors,

a farmer and a weaver.

"Promise me something," the farmer said.

"If I have a son and you have a daughter,

the two of them must marry.

That way, your land will be joined with mine."

The weaver agreed, but later she was sorry

for her promise.

4

Soon after that, the farmer's wife had a son

and named him Tong.

The weaver had a daughter and named her Mai Nhia.

The weaver looked down at her beautiful baby.

"You must marry the one you choose, Mai Nhia,"

she whispered.

"I will protect you from my foolish promise."

But what could the poor weaver do?

She thought and thought.

At last she came up with a plan.

She dressed her baby in boys' clothes

and told everyone that Mai Nhia was a boy.

Mai Nhia and Tong grew up as friends.

When they were old enough,

they went away to school together.

Tong was a handsome boy, but he was lazy.

He did not read or study or go to class.

"School is hard work," he said.

"I'd rather go fishing or take a nap."

Mai Nhia loved to learn.

She loved reading and working with numbers.

She loved writing stories, poems, and riddles.

She studied hard and did well in every class.

All through school, Mai Nhia kept her secret.

No one knew she was really a girl.

When their school days ended,

they traveled home together.

By now they were old enough to marry.

Mai Nhia looked at Tong and thought,

"My friend would make a handsome husband.

Maybe it's time I let him guess the truth."

Tong was walking ahead of her on the road.

"I have a riddle for you," Mai Nhia said.

"Answer it and you will know a secret about me.

Are you ready to guess?"

Tong frowned. He did not like riddles.

Figuring them out was too much work.

"Here's the riddle," said Mai Nhia.

"Two birds are walking along a road.

The rooster walks in front. The hen follows behind."

Tong did not understand what Mai Nhia meant.

He shrugged and walked on.

Halfway home, Mai Nhia decided to try again.

"Here's an easier riddle," she said.

"Guess what it means.

Once there were two friends.

The big one was a man.

The small one was a woman."

"Oh, stop bothering me!" Tong said.

"To answer your silly riddle, I would have to think!

I don't like thinking! It makes my head ache!

I'd rather sleep!"

"I could never marry such a foolish man!"

Mai Nhia thought.

When Mai Nhia got home, she dressed as a woman.

Tong was amazed when he saw her.

He wanted to marry her, but it was too late.

Mai Nhia no longer wanted to be his wife.

Mai Nhia was so clever and charming

that many young men came to court her.

She chose the finest one to be her husband.

Tong was angry.

"Why did you break your promise?"

he asked Mai Nhia's mother.

"Mai Nhia should have married me!"

"I wanted Mai Nhia to make her own choice,"

Mai Nhia's mother replied.

"You could have won her heart,

but you were foolish and did not educate yourself."

Tong's spirit grew very black.

"If I can't marry Mai Nhia, I will live alone!" he said.

He left his family and went off by himself.

Because he had not learned to read, write, or think,

he spent his days as a common worker

with nothing of his own.

But Mai Nhia, who had studied hard and learned well,

enjoyed a rich and happy life.